TAG Program
New Haven Public Schools
School_____
Teacher_____
Date_____ | Borrower's Name

For Mirko

Editors: Ann Redpath, Etienne Delessert
Art Director: Rita Marshall
Publisher: George R. Peterson, Jr.
Copyright © 1983 Creative Education, Inc., 123 S. Broad Street,
Mankato, Minnesota 56001, USA. American Edition.
Copyright © 1983 Grasset & Fasquelle, Paris – Editions 24 Heures, Lausanne. French Edition.
International copyrights reserved in all countries.
Library of Congress Catalog Card No.: 83-71179
Andersen, Hans Christian; The Fir Tree
Mankato, MN: Creative Education, Inc.; 32 pages. ISBN: 0-87191-949-4
Printed in Switzerland by Imprimeries Réunies S.A. Lausanne.

# THE FIRTREE

HANS CHRISTIAN ANDERSEN
illustrated by
MARCEL IMSAND
RITA MARSHALL

CREATIVE EDUCATION INC.

# ONCE UPON A TIME

THERE was a pretty little fir tree living in a wood. It was in an excellent position, for it could get sun, and there was enough air, and all around grew many tall companions, both pines and firs. The little fir tree's greatest desire was to grow up.

It did not heed the warm sun and the fresh air, or notice the little peasant children who ran about chattering when they came out to gather wild strawberries and raspberries. Often they found a whole basketful and strung strawberries on a straw; they would sit down by the little fir tree and say, "What a pretty little one this is!" The tree did not like that at all.

By the next year it had grown a whole ring taller, and the year after that another ring more, for you can always tell a fir tree's age from its rings.

"Oh, if I were only a great tree like the others," sighed the little fir tree, "then I could stretch out my branches far and wide and look out into the great world! The birds would build their nests in my branches, and when the wind blew I would bow to it politely just like the others!"

It took no pleasure in the sunshine, nor in the birds, nor in the rose-colored clouds that sailed over it at dawn and at sunset.

Then the winter came, and the snow lay white and sparkling all around, and a hare would come and spring right over the little fir tree, which annoyed it very much. But when two more winters had passed the fir tree was so tall that the hare had to run round it. "Ah, to grow and grow, and become great and old! That is the only pleasure in life," thought the tree.

In the autumn the woodcutters used to come and cut some of the tallest trees. This happened every year, and the young fir tree would shiver as the magnificent trees fell crashing and crackling to the ground, their branches hewn off, and the great trunks left bare, so that they were almost unrecognizable. But then they were laid on wagons and dragged out of the wood by horses. "Where are they going? What will happen to them?"

In spring, when the swallows and storks came, the fir tree asked them:

"Do you know where they were taken? Have you met them?"

The swallows knew nothing of them, but the stork nodded his head thoughtfully, saying:

"I think I know. I met many new ships as I flew from Egypt; there were splendid masts on the ships. I'll wager those were they! They had the scent of fir trees. Ah, those are grand, grand!"

"Oh, if I were only big enough to sail away over the sea too! What sort of thing is the sea? What does it look like?"

"Oh, it would take much too long to tell you all that," said the stork, and off he went.

"Rejoice in your youth," said the sunbeams, "rejoice in the sweet growing time, in the young life within you."

And the wind kissed it and the dew wept tears over it, but the fir tree did not understand.

Towards Christmastime quite little trees were cut down, some not as big as the young fir tree, or just the same age, and now it had no peace or rest for longing to be away. These little trees, which were chosen for their beauty, kept all their branches; they were put into carts and drawn out of the wood by horses.

"Where are those going?" asked the fir tree. "They are no bigger than I, and one there was much smaller even! Why do they keep their branches? Where are they taken to?"

"We know! We know!" twittered the sparrows. "Down there in the city we have peeped in at the windows, we know where they go! They come to the greatest splendor and magnificence you can imagine! We have looked in at the windows and seen them planted in the middle of the warm room and adorned with the most beautiful things — golden apples, sweetmeats, toys and hundreds of candles."

"And then?" asked the fir tree, trembling in every limb, "and then? What happens then?"

"Oh, we haven't seen anything more than that. That was simply matchless!"

"Am I also destined to the same brilliant career?" wondered the fir tree excitedly. "That is even better than sailing over the sea! I am sick with longing. If it were only Christmas! Now I am tall and grown-up like those which were taken away last year. Ah, if I were only in the cart! If I were only in the warm room with all the splendor and magnificence! And then? Then comes something better, something still more beautiful, else why should they dress us up? There must be something greater, something grander to come — but what? Oh! I am pining away! I really don't know what is the matter with me!"

"Rejoice in us," said the air and sunshine, "rejoice in your fresh youth in the free air!"

But it took no notice, and just grew and grew; there it stood fresh and green in winter and in summer, and all who saw it said, "What a beautiful tree!"

At Christmastime it was the first to be cut down. The axe went deep into the pith. The tree fell to the ground with a groan; it felt bruised and faint. It could not think of happiness, it was sad at leaving its home, the spot where it had sprung up; it knew, too, that it would never see again its dear old companions, or the little shrubs and flowers, perhaps not even the birds.

Altogether the parting was not pleasant.

When the tree came to itself again it was packed in a yard with other trees, and a man was saying:

"This is a splendid one, we shall only want this."

Then came a footman in uniform and carried the fir tree into a large and beautiful room. There were pictures hanging upon the walls, and near the Dutch stove stood great Chinese vases with lions on their lids. There were armchairs, silk-covered sofas, big tables laden with picture-books and toys, worth hundreds of pounds—at least, so the children said. The fir tree was placed in a great tub filled with sand, but no one could see that it was a tub, for it was all hung with greenery and stood on a colorful carpet. How the tree trembled! What was coming now? The young ladies and the servants decked it out. On its branches they hung little nets cut out of colored paper, each full of sugarplums. Gilt apples and nuts hung down as if they were growing, and over a hundred red, blue, and white candles were fastened among the branches. Dolls as lifelike as human beings—the fir tree had never seen any before—were suspended among the green, and right up at the top was fixed a golden star. It was gorgeous, quite unusually gorgeous!

"Tonight," they all said, "tonight it will be lighted!"

"Ah," thought the tree, "if it were only evening! Then the candles would soon be lighted. What will happen then? I wonder whether the trees will come from the wood to see me, or if the sparrows will fly against the window panes? Am I to stand here decked out thus through winter and summer?"

It was not a bad guess, but the fir tree had real bark-ache from sheer longing, and bark-ache in trees is just as bad as headache in human beings.

Now the candles were lighted. What a glitter! What splendor! The tree quivered in all its branches so much, that one of the candles caught the green, and singed it. "Take care!" cried the young ladies, and they extinguished it.

Now the tree did not even dare to quiver. It was really terrible! It was so afraid of losing any of its ornaments, and it was quite bewildered by all the radiance.

And then the folding doors were opened, and a crowd of children rushed in, as though they wanted to knock down the whole tree, while the older people followed soberly. The children stood quite silent, but only for a moment, and then they shouted again, and danced round the tree, and snatched off one present after another.

"What are they doing?" thought the tree. "What is going to happen?" And the candles burnt low on the branches, and were put out one by one, and then the children were given permission to plunder the tree. They rushed at it so that all its boughs creaked; if it had not been fastened by the gold star at the top to the ceiling, it would have been knocked over.

The children danced about with their splendid toys, and no one looked at the tree, except the old nurse, who came and peeped among the boughs, just to see if a fig or an apple had been forgotten.

"A story, a story!" cried the children, and dragged a little stout man to the tree. He sat down beneath it, saying, "Here we are in the greenwood, and the tree will be delighted to listen! But I am only going to tell one story. Shall it be Henny Penny or Humpty Dumpty who fell downstairs, and yet gained great honor and married a Princess?"

"Henny Penny!" cried some: "Humpty Dumpty!" cried others; there was a perfect babel of voices! Only the fir tree kept silent, and thought, "Am I not to be in it? Am I to have nothing to do with it?"

But the fir tree had already been in it, and played out its part. And the man told them about Humpty Dumpty who fell downstairs and married a princess. The children clapped their hands and cried, "Another, another!" They wanted the story of Henny Penny also, but they only got Humpty Dumpty. The fir tree stood quite astonished and thoughtful: the birds in the wood had never related anything like that. "Humpty Dumpty fell downstairs and yet married a princess! Yes, that is the way of the world," thought the tree, and was sure it must be true, because such a nice man had told the story. "Well, who knows? Perhaps I shall fall downstairs and marry a princess." And it rejoiced to think that next day it would be decked out again with candles, toys, glittering ornaments, and fruits. "Tomorrow I shall quiver again with excitement. I shall enjoy to the full all my splendor. Tomorrow I shall hear Humpty Dumpty again, and perhaps Henny Penny too." And the tree stood silent and lost in thought all through the night.

Next morning the servants came in. "Now the dressing up will begin again," thought the tree. But they dragged it out of the room, and up the stairs to the attic, and put it in a dark corner, where no ray of light could penetrate. "What does this mean?" thought the tree. "What am I to do here? What is there for me to hear?" And it leaned against the wall, and thought and thought. And there was time enough for that, for days and nights went by, and no one came. At last when someone did come, it was only to put some great boxes into the corner. Now the tree was quite covered; it seemed as if it had been quite forgotten.

"Now it is winter outdoors," thought the fir tree. "The ground is hard and covered with snow, they can't plant me yet, and that is why I am staying here under cover till the spring comes. How thoughtful they are! Only I wish it were not so terribly dark and lonely here; not even a little hare! It was so nice out in the wood, when the snow lay all around, and the hare leaped past me; yes, even when he leaped over me, but I didn't like it then. It's so dreadfully lonely up here."

"Squeak, squeak!" said a little mouse, stealing out, followed by a second. They sniffed at the fir tree, and then crept between its boughs. "It's frightfully cold," said the little mice. "How nice it is to be here! Don't you think so too, you old fir tree?"

"I'm not at all old," said the tree; "there are many much older than I am."

"Where do you come from?" asked the mice, "and what do you know?" They were extremely inquisitive. "Do tell us about the most beautiful place in the world. Is that where you come from? Have you been in the storeroom, where cheeses lie on the shelves, and hams hang from the ceiling, where one dances on tallow candles, and where one goes in thin and comes out fat?"

"I know nothing about that," said the tree. "But I know the wood, where the sun shines, and the birds sing." And then it told them all about its young days, and the little mice had never heard anything like that before, and they listened with all their ears, and said: "Oh, how much you have seen! How lucky you have been!"

"I?" said the fir tree, and then it thought over what it had told them. "Yes, on the whole those were very happy times." But then it went on to tell them about Christmas Eve, when it had been adorned with sweetmeats and candles.

"Oh!" said the little mice.

"How lucky you have been, you old fir tree!"

"I'm not at all old," said the tree. "I only came from the wood this winter. I am only a little backward, perhaps, in my growth."

"How beautifully you tell stories!" said the little mice. And next evening they came with four others, who wanted to hear the tree's story, and it told still more, for it remembered everything so clearly and thought, "Those were happy times! But they may come again. Humpty Dumpty fell downstairs, and yet he married a princess; perhaps I shall also marry a princess!" And then it thought of a pretty little birch tree that grew out in the wood, and seemed to the fir tree a real princess, and a very beautiful one too.

"Who is Humpty Dumpty?" asked the little mice.

And then the tree told the whole story. It could remember every single word, and the little mice were ready to leap on to the topmost branch out of sheer joy!

Next night many more mice came, and on Sunday even two rats; but they did not care about the story, and that troubled the little mice, because now they thought less of it too.

"Is that the only story you know?" asked the rats.

"The only one," answered the tree. "I heard that on my happiest evening, but I did not realize then how happy I was."

"That is a very poor story. Don't you know one about bacon or tallow candles? A storeroom story?"

"No," said the tree.

"Then we are much obliged to you," said the rats, and they went back to their friends.

At last the little mice went off also, and the tree said, sighing: "Really it was very pleasant when the lively little mice sat round and listened while I told them stories. But now that's over too. But now I will think of the time when I shall be brought out again, to keep up my spirits."

But when did that happen? Well, it was one morning when they came to tidy up the attic; the boxes were set aside, and the tree brought out. They threw it really rather roughly on the floor, but a servant dragged it off at once downstairs, where there was daylight once more.

"Now life begins again," thought the tree. It felt the fresh air, the first rays of the sun, and there it was out in the yard! Everything passed so quickly; the tree quite forgot to notice itself, there was so much to look at all around. The yard opened on a garden full of flowers; the roses were so fresh and sweet, hanging over a little trellis. The lime trees were in blossom, and the swallows flew about, saying, "Quirre-virre-vit, my husband has come home." But it was not the fir tree they meant.

"Now I shall live," thought the tree joyfully, stretching out its branches wide. But, alas, they were all withered and yellow; and it was lying in a corner among weeds and nettles. The golden star was still on its highest bough, and it glittered in the bright sunlight. In the yard some of the merry children were playing, who had danced so happily round the tree at Christmas. One of the little ones ran up, and tore off the gold star.

"Look what was left on the ugly old fir tree!" he cried, and stamped on the boughs so that they cracked under his feet.

And the tree looked at all the splendor and freshness of the flowers in the garden, and then looked at itself, and wished that it had been left lying in the dark corner of the attic; it thought of its fresh youth in the wood, of the merry Christmas Eve, and of the little mice who had listened so happily to the story of Humpty Dumpty.

"Too late! Too late!" thought the old tree. "If only I had enjoyed myself while I could. Now all is over and gone."

And a servant came and cut the tree into small pieces. There was quite a bundle of them; they flickered brightly under the great copper kettle. The tree sighed deeply, and each sigh was like a pistol shot; so the children who were playing there ran up, and sat in front of the fire, gazing at it, and crying, "Pfiff! puff! bang!" But for each report, which was really a sigh, the tree was thinking of a summer's day in the wood, or of a winter's night out there, when the stars were shining. It thought of Christmas Eve, and of Humpty Dumpty, which was the only story it had heard, or could tell, and then the tree burned away.

The children played on in the garden, and the youngest had the golden star on his breast, which the tree had worn on the happiest evening of its life. And now that was past—and the tree had passed away—and the story too, all ended and done with.

And that's the way with all stories!